Teacher's Book

The Last of the Mohicans

James Fenimore Cooper
retold by **Elizabeth Gray**

Express Publishing

Published by Express Publishing
Liberty House, New Greenham Park,
Newbury, Berkshire RG19 6HW
Tel: (0044) 1635 817 363 – Fax: (0044) 1635 817 463
e-mail: inquiries@expresspublishing.co.uk
http://www.expresspublishing.co.uk

First published 2000
New edition 2002

ISBN   1-84216-792-8

Contents

Introduction to the Teacher

Introductory Lesson

This introductory lesson is intended to stimulate the students' interest in the reader. By doing the 'Before reading' activities of lesson one, you will allow students to make suggestions about the plot. At this point, it does not matter whether the students' ideas are right or wrong, as long as they are based on evidence (pictures or chapter titles).

Following lessons

Pre-teach vocabulary in the last five minutes of the lesson in preparation for the following lesson.

Prepare the vocabulary for the next lesson as follows:

a) First read the vocabulary aloud so that the students can hear the pronunciation.
b) Students repeat chorally and individually.
c) Check individual pronunciation by having students repeat possible problem items.

Beginning with lesson one, each chapter may be prepared as follows:

1 Ss' books closed. Present the **Listening** activity for Ss to complete while they listen to the chapter on the recording for the first time.
2 Ss report back their answers to the listening activity.
3 Ss open their books. Play the recording again and Ss follow the lines. Pause - Ss repeat selected sections chorally and/or individually.
4 Let your Ss read aloud paragraph by paragraph. Check and correct Ss' pronunciation while they are reading.
5 Ask the **Comprehension questions** for the unit.
6 Do the **Topics for discussion** for the unit - encourage Ss to talk about their own experiences.
7 Present the **Activity/Activities** for the unit.
8 Pre-teach vocabulary for the next chapter.

NB: **Vocabulary Exercises.** These are at the end of each chapter (i.e. Lesson One - Chapter One **Vocabulary Exercises**). We suggest that these be set as homework, but if there is time they can be started in class. Ss may refer to the text in order to complete the exercises.

INTRODUCTORY LESSON

About the author:

1 **1** The United States
   2 11
   3 Yale
   4 1826
   5 1851

2 **1** **a)** French troops   **d)** Indian camps
   b) Fort Edward   **e)** Fort Henry
   c) forest   **f)** waterfall

   2 The Iroquois, the Hurons, the Mohicans and the Delawares.
   3 Major Heyward, Cora, Alice and Magua.

LESSON ONE - CHAPTER 1

I Listening

1 north-east   **5** friendly   **8** from
2 fighting   **6** English   **9** short
3 area   **7** river   **10** beard
4 everywhere

II Comprehension questions

1 Because there were enemy soldiers and dangerous Indians.
2 The French troops were moving south.

3 To take a thousand men and fight off the French.
4 His daughters; Cora and Alice.
5 He thought it was too dangerous.
6 Through the forest.

III Topics for discussion

Ss' own answers

IV Activities

A 1 Major Heyward   4 General Webb
    2 Alice   5 Cora
    3 Magua

B

General appearance	handsome
Height	tall, short
Build	small, powerful
Hair	curly, blond, black, ponytail, long, white
Other features	rosy cheeks, bald head, white beard, darker skin

C Ss' own answers

Vocabulary Exercises

I 1 uniform   3 silent   5 forest
    2 knee   4 touch

II	1 extremely	3 protection	5 completely
	2 friendly	4 safe	

III	1 off	3 with	5 up
	2 back	4 for	

IV	1 bushes	4 mountains	7 leaf
	2 singer	5 nature	8 shirt
	3 pipe	6 ride	

LESSON TWO - CHAPTER 2

I Listening

1 T   2 F   3 T   4 F   5 T

II Comprehension questions

1 They rode horses.
2 David Gamut.
3 They didn't know where they were.
4 Two Indians and a white man dressed in animal skins.
5 Indians who helped the white soldiers.
6 A loud Indian scream, then a gunshot.

III Topics for discussion

Ss' own answers

IV Activities

A i)   a) hat, shirt, trousers, boots, scarf
      b) dress, coat, shoes
      c) skirt, jacket, blouse
  ii) trousers, boots, shoes

B Major Heyward is wearing black boots, white trousers, a white shirt and a red jacket.
Alice is wearing a purple skirt and a purple blouse.
Cora is wearing a blue skirt and a blue blouse.
Gamut is wearing black boots, white trousers, a white shirt, a brown jacket and a green hat.

C **1** d   **3** e   **5** b   **7** g
    2 f   **4** h   **6** c   **8** a

Ss' own answers

Vocabulary Exercises

I **1** handmade   **4** ride   **7** have
   2 grey   **5** deer-skin   **8** loud
   3 thick   **6** secret

II **1** A   **2** B   **3** B   **4** C   **5** A

III **1** back   **3** in
    2 under   **4** up

IV **1** wolf   **4** waterfall   **7** neck
    2 canoe   **5** world   **8** shoulder
    3 gift   **6** tomahawk

LESSON THREE - CHAPTER 3

I Listening

1 B   **2** A   **3** C   **4** C   **5** B

II Comprehension questions

1 Two.
2 Magua threw his tomahawk at them.
3 In the Mohicans' secret hiding place.
4 Jump into the water.
5 To be with Cora.

III Topics for discussion

    Ss' own answers

IV Activities

A 1 Wolf.
   2 Three groups.
   3 The women took care of the homes and fields while the men hunted and fished.
   4 The villages were large and built on hills.
   5 The council met regularly to discuss important matters.
   6 Today Mohicans live in Wisconsin and are called Stockbridge Indians.

B Ss' own answers

Vocabulary Exercises

I
1	b	**3**	d	**5**	c
2	e	**4**	f	**6**	a

II
1	howl	**3**	followed	**5**	ground
2	express	**4**	capture	**6**	entrance

III
1	out	**4**	to	**7**	to
2	at	**5**	like	**8**	like
3	off	**6**	at		

IV
1	deer	**3**	marry	**5**	scared
2	prisoner	**4**	council	**6**	blanket

LESSON FOUR - CHAPTER 4

I Listening

1	arm	**3**	deer	**5**	tomahawk
2	Hurons	**4**	Cora		

II Comprehension questions

1 Magua.
2 Back to the forest.
3 To tell the other Indians they had prisoners.
4 To marry him.

5 Tied them to trees.
6 Hawkeye.

III Topics for discussion

Ss' own answers

IV Activities

A Ss' own answers

B 1 ✗   3 ✓   5 ✗   7 ✗
   2 ✗   4 ✗   6 ✓   8 ✗

C 1 First   3 After that/Then
   2 Then/After that 4 Finally

Vocabulary Exercises

I
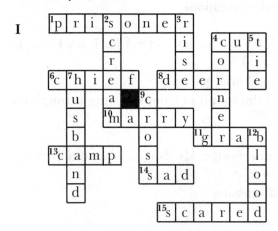

II **1** frightened   **3** beautiful   **5** yelled
       2 come back   **4** took

III **1** to   **2** to   **3** off   **4** at   **5** away

IV Ss' own answers

LESSON FIVE - CHAPTER 5

I Listening

1 Alice = Cora
2 Fort Edward = Fort Henry
3 dark = foggy
4 enemies = soldiers
5 sitting = standing

II Comprehension questions

1 "He is the clever fox, but if the clever fox is not killed, he will return to kill."
2 The Mohicans' burial ground.
3 Gunfire and the sound of troops moving through the forest.
4 It was foggy.
5 "Lower the drawbridge! My daughters are out there."

III Topics for discussion

Ss' own answers

IV Activities

A i) **1** c   **3** b   **5** d
     2 e   **4** a

   ii) **Ss' own answers**

B   Iroquois Indian = Huron Indian
    opera singer = church singer
    jungle = forest
    General Webb = Uncas
    safe = dangerous
    knife = tomahawk
    day = night
    hut = cave
    Huron Indians = Iroquois Indians
    Major Heyward = Hawkeye

Vocabulary Exercises

I   **1** C   **2** A   **3** B   **4** A   **5** A

II   **1** b   **2** c   **3** a

III   **1** by   **2** on   **3** in   **4** of   **5** down

IV   **Ss' own answers**

LESSON SIX - CHAPTER 6

I Listening

1 F   **2** F   **3** T   **4** T   **5** T

II Comprehension questions

1 Five days.
2 To discuss the surrender.
3 That nobody would hurt his daughters.
4 At the front leading the troops.
5 Magua.
6 He took them both away.

III Topics for discussion

Ss' own answers

IV A i) **1** B   **2** A   **3** D   **4** C

ii) **1)** In a small hut.
2) Arrows.
3) A herd of buffaloes.
4) A coyote.
5) A lot of arrows.

B Ss' own answers

Vocabulary Exercises

I   **1** interest   **3** promise   **5** look
    2 surrender **4** kidnap

II **1** B   **2** A   **3** B   **4** B   **5** A

III **Ss' own answers**

LESSON SEVEN - CHAPTER 7

I Listening

1 area   **2** ground **3** found   **4** strange **5** head

II Comprehension questions

1 Cora's green scarf.
2 Signs such as broken tree branches and footprints.
3 In two canoes.
4 He looked for signs of the Huron Indians.
5 Uncas.

III Topics for discussion

   Ss' own answers

IV Activities

A

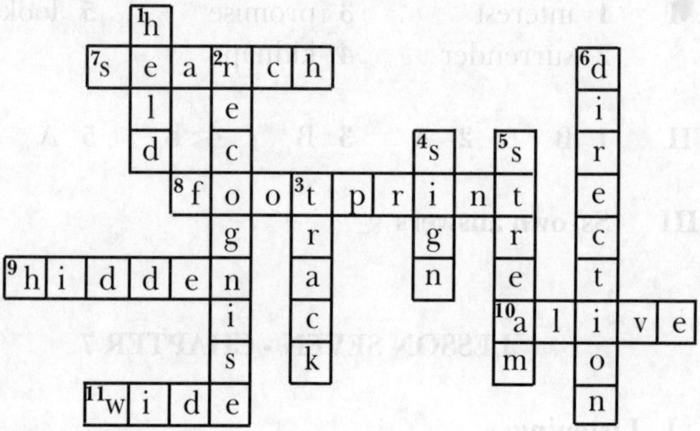
1 held
2 recognise
3 track
4 sign
5 stream
6 direction
7 search
8 footprint
9 hidden
10 alive
11 wide

B Ss' own answers

C Ss' own answers

Vocabulary Exercises

I

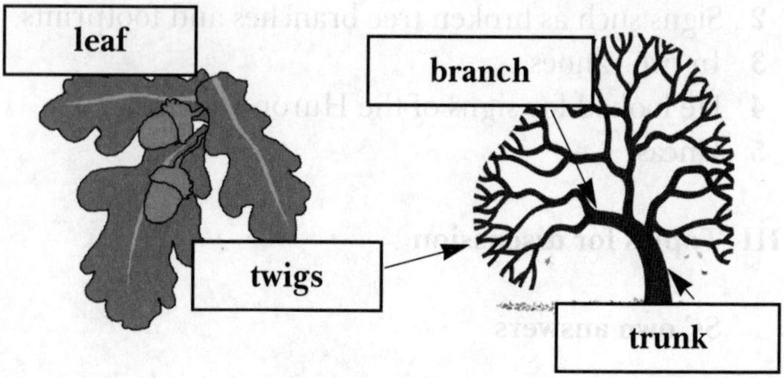
leaf
branch
twigs
trunk

II **1** lost **3** while **5** tightly
    2 dark **4** wearing

III **1** out **2** about **3** off **4** around

IV **Ss' own answers**

LESSON EIGHT - CHAPTER 8

I Listening

1 c **2** e **3** a **4** d **5** b

II Comprehension questions

1 With different Indian tribes.
2 Because they thought the way he sang was crazy.
3 Go with Gamut to the Indian's camp.
4 To help a sick Indian woman.
5 In a cave.
6 Hawkeye.
7 Guard the cave.

III Topics for discussion

Ss' own answers

IV Activities

A **1** a **3** a **5** a **7** c
    2 b **4** c **6** c

B 1) Good morning, Melissa.
2) What seems to be the problem?
3) Oh, dear! How did it happen?
4) OK. Let me have a look at it.
5) It's nothing serious but you should rest it for the next few days.

C Ss' own answers

Vocabulary Exercises

| **I** | **1** huge | **3** sick | **5** bear |
| | **2** feed | **4** lie | **6** fever |

II	**1** honour	**4** respect	**7** guard
	2 carry	**5** ridiculous	**8** responsible
	3 familiar	**6** roared	

| **III** | **1** in | **3** At | **5** for |
| | **2** down | **4** in | **6** for |

| **IV** | **1** dance | **3** sign | **5** shines |
| | **2** teepee | **4** turtle | **6** hunt |

LESSON NINE - CHAPTER 9

I Listening

1 U   2 T   3 H   4 M   5 C

II   Comprehension questions

1 His grandfather was a Delaware.
2 He had tattoos on his face.
3 She was Magua's prisoner.
4 "Take me, instead."
5 One day.
6 He sang and danced a war dance.

III Topics for discussion

Ss' own answers

IV Activities

1	must	3	mustn't	5	can
2	must	4	mustn't	6	mustn't

Vocabulary Exercises

I	1 until		3 carefully		5 lie
	2 really		4 great		

II	1 in	2 to	3 on	4 on	5 away

III	1 worst		3 careful		5 represent
	2 really		4 brightly		

IV   Ss' own answers

LESSON TEN - CHAPTER 10

I Listening

1 C   **2** B   **3** A   **4** A   **5** B

II Comprehension questions

1 To a cave, at the bottom of a mountain, behind a village.
2 Attack the village.
3 With a spear.
4 Hawkeye shot him.
5 They were buried next to each other.
6 "Chingachgook, you are not alone. I will go anywhere with you."
7 He was the last of the Mohicans.

III Topics for discussion

Ss' own answers

IV Activities

A i) **1** time   **3** death   **5** song
          2 hearts   **4** lives   **6** hero

     ii) b

B Ss' own answers

C Ss' own answers

Vocabulary Exercises

I **1** rises   **3** make   **5** lose
   2 let out   **4** aim   **6** bury

II **1** B   **3** B   **5** A
   2 A   **4** C   **6** C

III **1** to   **3** on   **5** onto
   2 of   **4** at

Test A

A   Listen to the recording and fill in the gaps. You will hear it twice.

Gamut had been **1)** .... in the leg, but it was not serious. He sat on a **2)** .... next to Cora and Alice, singing a sad song quietly to himself. Alice was terribly frightened by the **3)** .... She sat on the bed **4)** .... in Cora's arms. "I'm **5)** .... I want to get out of here."

"It's alright. Father's coming. We'll leave in the **6)** ...." An Indian had stabbed Major Heyward in the arm. His white shirt was now **7)** .... with blood. Heyward walked through the **8)** .... to see if there was another way out. He saw a big hole in the rock on the side of the **9)** .... and he heard Indian voices outside. He waited quietly, and when they **10)** ...., he returned to the others.

B   Circle the correct item.

1   The................ marched for six hours to meet their regiment.
   A troops   **B** bears   **C** singers

2   An Indian .... is the leader of the tribe.
   A prisoner   **B** soldier   **C** chief

3   "What are you wearing? You look absolutely..........!"
   A expressionless **B** ridiculous   **C** responsible

4   The council .... the problem yesterday.
   A discussed   **B** surrendered   **C** captured

5 After .... the princess the gang demanded money.

   A stealing   **B** hunting   **C** kidnapping

C   **Answer the following questions:**

1 Who is Cora and Alice's father? ....
2 What was the Mohican's secret hiding place? ....
3 What was Gamut? ....
4 Which side won the battle outside Fort Henry? ....
5 Who was the last of the Mohicans? ....

D   **Match the words in box A with their opposites from box B.**

	A		B
1	safe	**a**	well
2	elder	**b**	happiness
3	scream	**c**	dangerous
4	sick	**d**	whisper
5	sadness	**e**	younger

1 ....   **2** ....   **3** ....   **4** ....   **5** ....

E   **Who said what?**

1

"Lower the drawbridge! My daughters are out there."

2

"I came here to sing. Nature is the perfect place to hear music!"

3 "You cannot give my prisoner to someone else."

4 "It's alright, Alice. You're safe with Father now."

5 "Take me, instead I will give you my gun. You know how much you want to kill me."

1 .... **4** ....
2 .... **5** ....
3 ....

F Fill in the gaps with a word from the box.

| unconscious | trust | gunfire | shadow | enemy |

1 A dark .... made them scream in fear.

2 The .... went on until the soldiers had no more bullets left.

3 After the accident she was .... for an hour.

4 "Don't you ....me? I thought we were best friends."

5 "The .... is waiting for you in the forest. You must be very careful," said the General.

G Fill in the gaps with the correct preposition.

| on | in | at | up | about |

1 The fat ginger cat was asleep .... the carpet.

2 "Prices go .... every day," moaned Jane, "everything is so expensive!"

3 "It's .... the garden, where you left it yesterday," said their dad.

4 "You shouldn't care what people think .... you," she told him.

5 All his friends were waiting for him .... the restaurant.

H **Match the words with the definitions.**

1	teepee	**a**	very silly
2	alone	**b**	extremely wicked
3	prisoner	**c**	by yourself
4	evil	**d**	an Indian tent
5	foolish	**e**	someone who has been captured

1 .... **2** .... **3** .... **4** .... **5** ....

I **Fill in the gaps with a derivative of the word in bold.**

1 People should learn to .... their feelings.
expressionless

2 All the girls were wearing .... ribbons in their hair.
colour

3 The gold was .... behind the boxes.
hide

4 When the sun .... they saw the beautiful countryside.
rise

5 There was an .... in the cliff which looked like a cave.
open

Test B

A **Listen to the recording and fill in the gaps. You will hear it twice.**

Gamut had been shot in the **1)** ...., but it was not serious. He sat on a blanket next to Cora and Alice, **2)** .... a sad song quietly to himself. Alice was terribly **3)** .... by the fighting. She sat on the bed crying in Cora's **4)** ....

"I'm scared. I want to get out of **5)** ...."

"It's alright. Father's coming. We'll **6)** .... in the morning." An Indian had stabbed Major Heyward in the arm. His white shirt was now red with **7)** .... Heyward **8)** .... through the tunnels to see if there was another way out. He saw a big hole in the **9)** .... on the side of the mountain and he heard Indian voices outside. He waited quietly, and when they left, he **10)** .... to the others.

B **Circle the correct item.**

1 The Indian wore his hair in a ....
   A animal skin   **B** ponytail   **C** bush

2 Katy had a .... that something exciting would happen.
   A look   **B** choice   **C** feeling

3 I only received your .... today and I haven't had time to reply.
   A message   **B** search   **C** rope

4 A soldier's job is to .... their country.
   A protect   **B** promise   **C** surprise

5 Sarah .... held the newborn baby.
   A especially   **B** suddenly   **C** carefully

C   **Answer the following questions:**

1 Who is Chingachgook's son? ....
2 Which tribe of Indians was Magua from? ....
3 Who did Magua want to marry? ....
4 How long did Uncas have to wait before he could follow Magua and Cora? ....
5 What did Hawkeye pretend to be when Alice was rescued?
   ....

D   **Match the words in box A with their opposites from box B.**

A	B
1 deserted	**a** together
2 separate	**b** life
3 enemy	**c** disappear
4 appear	**d** busy
5 death	**e** friend

1 ....   2 ....   3 ....   4 ....   5 ....

E Who said what?

1 "I take the girl."

2 "I only ask that nobody hurts my daughters."

3 "Chingachgook, you are not alone."

4 "Save my sister, Alice. You've done enough for me."

5 "I'm scared. I want to get out of here."

1 ....   4 ....
2 ....   5 ....
3 ....

F Fill in the gaps with a word from the box

| almost | capture | faint | deserted | discuss |

1 We .... didn't catch the train.
2 They tried to .... the injured lion.
3 It is important to .... problems.
4 After the celebrations the streets were ....
5 Lucy felt very dizzy and thought that she might ....

G Fill in the gaps with the correct preposition

| on | in | to | up | about |

1 "Go .... the hill and you'll see the library on the right."

2 "I'm looking for the road .... the castle. Can you tell me where to go?"

3 "I hate questions .... geography."

4 The diamonds were .... a black suitcase.

5 They sat .... a rug to eat their picnic.

H Match the words with the definitions.

1	ridiculous	**a**	maybe
2	protect	**b**	to take something which is not your own
3	perhaps	**c**	crazy
4	herb	**d**	to look after something
5	steal	**e**	a small green plant

1 .... 2 .... 3 .... 4 .... 5 ....

I Fill in the gaps with a derivative of the word in bold.

1 She has the .... haircut I have ever seen!
worse

2 We .... washed the expensive glasses.
careful

3 I felt so .... when my dog died.
sadness

4 It's very .... tonight. I can't see anything!
fog

5 A very .... thing happened last night.
strangely

Key to Tests

NB: The listening section is taken from Chapter 4.

TEST A

A	**1** shot	**5** scared	**8** tunnels
	2 blanket	**6** morning	**9** mountain
	3 fighting	**7** red	**10** left
	4 crying		

B **1** A   **2** C   **3** B   **4** A   **5** C

C **1** Colonel Munro.   **3** A church singer.
 2 A cave behind a   **4** The French.
  waterfall.   **5** Chingachgook.

D **1** c   **2** e   **3** d   **4** a   **5** b

E **1** Colonel Munro   **4** Cora
 2 David Gamut   **5** Hawkeye
 3 Magua

F **1** shadow   **3** unconcious   **5** enemy
 2 gunfire   **4** trust

G **1** on   **2** up   **3** in   **4** about   **5** at

H **1** d   **2** c   **3** e   **4** b   **5** a

I **1** express   **3** hidden   **5** opening
 2 colourful   **4** rose

TEST B

A 1 leg   5 here   8 walked
2 singing   6 leave   9 rock
3 frightened   7 blood   10 returned
4 arms

B 1 B   2 C   3 A   4 A   5 C

C 1 Uncas.   4 One day.
2 The Huron.   5 A bear.
3 Cora.

D 1 d   2 a   3 e   4 c   5 b

E 1 Magua   4 Cora
2 Colonel Munro   5 Alice
3 Hawkeye

F 1 almost   3 discuss   5 faint
2 capture   4 deserted

G 1 up   2 to   3 about   4 in   5 on

H 1 c   2 d   3 a   4 e   5 b

I 1 worst   3 sad   5 strange
2 carefully   4 foggy

Suggested marking scheme:

A	10 items × 1 point per item =	10 points
B	5 items × 1 point per item =	5 points
C	5 items × 1 point per item =	5 points
D	5 items × 1 point per item =	5 points
E	5 items × 1 point per item =	5 points
F	5 items × 1 point per item =	5 points
G	5 items × 1 point per item =	5 points
H	5 items × 1 point per item =	5 points
I	5 items × 1 point per item =	5 points

Total: 50 points

$$50 \times 0.4 = 20$$